IN THE SLUSH

by Daniel Prillaman

GHOST LIGHT
PUBLICATIONS

IN THE SLUSH

SPECIAL NOTE

SPECIAL NOTE ON SONGS AND RECORDINGS

Cover Art and Book Design: Jonathan Cook
Second Edition: July 2025
ISBN 978-1-964045-02-3

IN THE SLUSH by Daniel Prillaman was a part of The Skeleton Rep(resents)' Craft Development Process in 2022. Dramaturgy was provided by Emily Claire Schmitt.

IN THE SLUSH received its world premiere at Le Chat Noir in Augusta, GA in July 2025. Produced by Gather by the Ghost Light. Directed by Jonathan Cook & Devon McSherry with stage manager Dixie Dawson. The cast was as follows:

LAURA BETH .... Korilyn Hendricks
ETHAN .... TJ Reissner
HOPE .... Karla Daly
HAROLD .... Brad King
SULTRY ANNOUNCER .... Amy Patton
BASSIST .... Brad Cannata

IN THE SLUSH

CHARACTERS

LAURA BETH GARDNER

30s, Any ethnicity, Female, Editorial Assistant, Wife of Ethan, Best Friend of Hope, Pregnant (does not need to be showing).

ETHAN GARDNER

30s, Any ethnicity, Male, Not an Editorial Assistant, Husband of Laura Beth, Friend of Hope.

HOPE ROSENSTOCK

30s, Any ethnicity, Female, Editorial Assistant, Best Friend of Laura Beth, Friend of Ethan.

<u>With special appearances by:</u>

RODINA WAITS

(As portrayed by Laura Beth Gardner) 30s, Any ethnicity, Female, Aspiring Poet (samples available upon request), Marital Status Unknown, Friend Status Unknown.

ORLANDO BOOM

(As portrayed by Ethan Gardner) Age Unknown, Any ethnicity, Male, Impossibly Sexual Interstellar Space Explorer, Marital Status [REDACTED].

HAROLD BECKLESBY

60s, Any ethnicity, Male, Marital Status Unknown

PLACE

The Gardner Household basement.

TIME

Recently.

AUTHOR NOTES

A spaced ellipsis in dialogue … with air on both sides represents unspoken words for the actor or a small beat. They may vary in length but do mark a momentary shift, pause, or silence.

"Like the boundless sea

You are colossal to me."

-Rodina Waits, *Untitled*

<u>**SCENE ONE**</u>

The Gardner Household basement.

Rugs, refurbished furniture, perhaps a paint job here and there cover the room, an ongoing attempt to hide or beautify the cinder block walls and concrete floor. The age of the space seeps through, but the naked eye largely sees it as intended, a comfortable haven for lounging and relaxation. Shelves of books and/or intricate, built models of various kinds line a wall. Maybe a beer fridge commands another.

On (and significantly around) a coffee table is a plethora of filled boxes, folders, and uncovered manuscripts. It's a rather striking amount of unread hopes and dreams.

There are two entrances/exits to the room: A single door on the basement level, leading to a side room, and another door stands unseen at the top of the stairwell running behind all the furniture and main set-up.

Currently, the side room door is open, and what is seen of the inside does little to reveal the room's function. Like the rest of the basement, there is evidence of redecoration and some repurposing. Presumably it was once a boiler or laundry room, maybe a bathroom, or even some combination of all three, but no longer.

No one is visible in the threshold, but perhaps there is some movement or shuffling from inside, disturbing the air enough to signify that someone is there, out of sight, doing whatever it is the room is for.

After a silence, the stairwell door opens and a pair of feet begins to descend the stairs.

Eventually, the body of Laura Beth Gardner reveals itself, carrying yet another box.

She grunts, the task not being particularly difficult, just awkward.

Hearing this toil, the head or top half of Ethan Gardner appears in the side room threshold.

ETHAN. Laura Beth?

LAURA BETH. I'm fine.

ETHAN. *(Crossing to help.)* Oh my god. I told you to let me help with those.

LAURA BETH. You did. And what did I say?

ETHAN. If I recall correctly, it was something along the lines of "over my left nut."

LAURA BETH. I believe it was exactly along those lines.

ETHAN. You know, I don't want to be that husband, but...

LAURA BETH. Husband! Oh, say that again.

ETHAN. Wife. I'm serious.

LAURA BETH. What? Just because I'm pregnant now I shouldn't be carrying heavy boxes?

ETHAN. Uh, exactly, along those lines. Yeah.

LAURA BETH. Hmm. But it's not like you're a doctor or anything, though.

ETHAN. Again. Uh...

LAURA BETH. Oh. *(Setting the box down on a stack.)* Ah. Yeah. Maybe you're right.

ETHAN. Are you okay?

LAURA BETH. I'm fine. You can't blame me for wanting to do as much as I can before I balloon.

ETHAN. No. I suppose I can't. But if there's more, you really should let me get them.

LAURA BETH. Relax. Hope's got the rest.

ETHAN. And you're going to let her carry all of it. Right?

LAURA BETH. That does not sound like a bad idea.

ETHAN. You are just too delicate for manual labor like that.

LAURA BETH. Oh, I am?

ETHAN. I worry about you.

LAURA BETH. Oh. That's so sweet. Look at you trying to be romantic but coming off mildly sexist.

ETHAN. What? Oh, I didn't mean it that way.

LAURA BETH. I'm messing with you, baby. But it is a good thing you're pretty.

ETHAN. It is. I am very lucky.

(They kiss.)

LAURA BETH. Remind me why I just married you?

ETHAN. Because you love me.

LAURA BETH. I do love you.

(They kiss.)

ETHAN. I love you, too.

LAURA BETH. Ugh. *(looking around at all the boxes)* Tell me I don't regret this already.

ETHAN. Hah. If I could save you, I would.

LAURA BETH. You can save me. Pick up a stack, start reading.

ETHAN. You know, I would. But I'm on call, and I've got

to keep my head clear.

LAURA BETH. Oh, you can't do that by reading.

ETHAN. Too many words. You understand.

LAURA BETH. Mmmhmm. It is a good thing you're pretty.

ETHAN. It is.

(They kiss.)

LAURA BETH. My hero.

ETHAN. Here. I'll tell you what I can do.

(He pats a couch and sits.)

Let me see those feet.

LAURA BETH. Oh my god.

(She sits and removes her shoes, then lays her feet on Ethan's lap. He massages her feet as she relaxes over the following.)

Ohhhhhhh. My hero. Mmmmmm. Ooh, ah.

ETHAN. You all right?

LAURA BETH. Very. You spoil me.

ETHAN. Only when you let me.

LAURA BETH. Mmm.

(Ethan stops briefly, staring at Laura Beth's feet.)

Noooo. Why'd you stop?

ETHAN. Sorry--your toes.

LAURA BETH. What about them?

ETHAN. I've never noticed this before, your middle toes, they're--connected.

LAURA BETH. Only halfway.

ETHAN. Have they always been like that?

LAURA BETH. Yeah. I'm a fish. I didn't tell you?

ETHAN. No, this is news. My parents forbade me from marrying fish.

LAURA BETH. Oh. Screw 'em, then.

ETHAN. *(laughs)* I just--can't believe I never noticed that. I should have noticed that.

LAURA BETH. What do you mean, should have?

ETHAN. ... I usually notice things like that.

LAURA BETH. Uh-huh. It's not that uncommon. There's a word for it. I forget what it is. But there's a word for it.

ETHAN. Yeah?

LAURA BETH. I think it starts with an "S?"

ETHAN. It's all right. Don't worry about it.

LAURA BETH. Sin... something. I don't know.

(Ethan kisses her feet and continues the massage.)

ETHAN. Shhhh.

LAURA BETH. Mmmmm.

(Beat.)

How's the model coming along?

ETHAN. What? Oh. Good. It's coming along.

LAURA BETH. You gonna let me see it?

ETHAN. When it's done.

LAURA BETH. Yeah. All right.

ETHAN. You okay?

LAURA BETH. ... I'll just say it. I know you're not meaning to, but the way you act about that room, it's a little Bluebeard-y.

ETHAN. A little who?

LAURA BETH. You really don't read, do you?

ETHAN. I'm more of a documentary guy.

LAURA BETH. *(chiming in with Ethan)* "I'm more of a documentary guy." Bluebeard. Wealthy nobleman, married many times, but his wives always have the strangest habit of vanishing under mysterious circumstances. One day, before he leaves for a trip, he gives his newest wife keys to every room in his regal, gigantic mansion. But he orders her to stay out of one particular room in the basement. So naturally, that's exactly what she doesn't do. She unlocks the basement room door, overcome by desire and curiosity, and what does she find but the bloody bodies of all the missing former wives, hanging from hooks on the walls.

ETHAN. Uh-huh. So you think I've got dead bodies hanging in there?

LAURA BETH. I'm not saying that. I am saying you've never really let me inside to see.

ETHAN. *(chuckles)* If you want to go in and look around, you can. There's not much to see. Just worktables and tools.

LAURA BETH. Really? I would have to get up then, wouldn't I?

ETHAN. You would.

LAURA BETH. Well, maybe in a little while, then.

(They kiss. She revels in Ethan's eyes.)

ETHAN. What?

LAURA BETH. I'm just so happy.

ETHAN. I am, too.

(Perhaps another kiss, as Ethan's hand finds its way to Laura Beth's belly. Laura Beth places her hands on top.)

ETHAN. What about Jude?

LAURA BETH. Jude?

ETHAN. Yeah.

LAURA BETH. Little archaically Biblical, don't you think?

ETHAN. No, it's not.

LAURA BETH. Besides, what makes you so sure she's going to be a boy?

ETHAN. You think it's a girl?

LAURA BETH. I know she's a girl. I've already decided.

ETHAN. Pretty sure that's not how it works.

LAURA BETH. It is. Guinevere.

ETHAN. Guinevere?

LAURA BETH. Mmmhmm.

ETHAN. And you think Jude is archaic?

LAURA BETH. It's the good kind of archaic.

ETHAN. Guinevere Gardner.

LAURA BETH. Gwen for short. Good, right? Yep, there it is.

ETHAN. The alliteration.

LAURA BETH. I thought you'd like that.

ETHAN. That's--?

LAURA BETH. King Arthur.

ETHAN. Nerd.

LAURA BETH. You love it.

ETHAN. I do.

> *(They kiss.)*

LAURA BETH. And, hey, by the time I'm done with all this, she'll be here. Get ready.

ETHAN. I sincerely hope it doesn't take that long. I would still like to see you before she comes.

LAURA BETH. Look at it all. I die a little inside just looking at it.

ETHAN. I still can't believe you convinced Barry to let you bring the entire thing here.

LAURA BETH. I still can't believe Barry insists on submissions in hard copy.

ETHAN. That too.

LAURA BETH. We sweet talked him, that's how. Hope and I told him, "If we've got the weekend to trim the pile and find a needle of bare minimum competency in a haystack, there's no way we're doing it in the damn office." I believe the phrase "over my left nut" was used.

ETHAN. There's got to be something good in here.

LAURA BETH. I'm sure there is. It's just the matter of finding it. That part's... less fun.

ETHAN. Is it really that bad?

LAURA BETH. Some of this stuff you have to see to believe. There are gems, but they're buried beneath so so much crap. Worse than crap. Not even "so bad, it's good" crap, just "so bad, it's bad" crap.

ETHAN. Well, crap. All part of the dream, huh?

LAURA BETH. All part of the dream. When you do finally find what you're looking for? You're holding it in your hands, buzzing from the energy it's giving? You've found the creation you're going to help somebody share with everyone. That's why we do it. That's the pep talk they give us. But... it is a good feeling.

ETHAN. ... Well. You got this. It'll be over before you know it.

LAURA BETH. That is a lie.

ETHAN. Rue Britannia.

LAURA BETH. Rule Britannia?

ETHAN. King Arthur.

LAURA BETH. That was so after.

ETHAN. Excalibur.

LAURA BETH. Oh my god. I love you.

ETHAN. I love you, too.

LAURA BETH. Thanks for helping.

ETHAN. You barely let me.

LAURA BETH. Hope's coming over probably about 8?

ETHAN. All right. You just shout if I can get you anything, okay?

LAURA BETH. Wine?

ETHAN. No wine.

LAURA BETH. No wine. *(to her belly)* You little bastard, you couldn't show up a week later?

ETHAN. Guinevere.

LAURA BETH. See?

ETHAN. I'll make you some tea.

(He crosses and closes the side room door, then begins climbing the stairs.)

LAURA BETH. Teaaaaaaaa.

ETHAN. Maybe order a pizza.

LAURA BETH. No pineapple!

ETHAN. We'll see.

LAURA BETH. Don't you dare! It is a cardinal sin!

(Ethan is gone. Laura Beth looks around at all the

boxes, steeling herself for the task ahead. Beat. Then, suddenly yelling up after Ethan.)

Syndactyly! … That's the word. Syndactyly. Weird little word. *(to her belly)* Strap in, Gwen. It's gonna be a bumpy ride.

(She grabs a stack of papers and/or a box and gets comfortable. But before she really starts reading, she looks over at the side room door. Beat. She stands, crosses to the door, and turns the knob. It does not turn. The door is locked. Beat. She returns to her previous spot and begins to read.)

The lights fade.

<u>SCENE TWO</u>

In the darkness, with a combination of laughter and pitying amusement, the voice of Hope Rosenstock reads aloud a section of manuscript.

During her speech, lights rise, revealing the same basement, later that evening. The main clues to the passage of time being Hope's presence, an empty pizza box or two, teacups, wine bottles and glasses, and many shuffled papers.

HOPE. *(reading)* "The paint splattered her barest essence. My fingers brushed her skin, and her nipples surged outward, hardening in the ultraviolet light. My penis quivered with jubilant glee."

LAURA BETH. Oh god.

HOPE. *(reading)* "The expectation. The anticipation. This was it. The moment I had been waiting for. That I had dreamed of since I was a child. I was about to conquer a Colactian. Or was it she who was about to conquer me? I stared into her six eyes, each of which looked back at me, into my soul, piercing me deeper than any gaze I've ever known. Again I pulsated in my sex. I reached for my manhood and began to stroke. 'Stop,' she said, a tentacle rising naughtily above her shoulder. 'You will not cum. You will not even touch your cock unless I give you permission. Is that understood?' Oh gods yes. YES. I understand. 'I understand,' I nearly shouted. 'Good,' she uttered. 'Now lie down. On your belly.' I obeyed, and her moist tentacles slathered over my backside, entering the cavernous, gaping opening of my--

LAURA BETH. Stooooop! Oh my god!

HOPE. God, LB, it gets so much better!

LAURA BETH. I'll take your word for it.

HOPE. I think we've got a winner here.

LAURA BETH. I will admit. It's certainly much more colorful than this "we're all living in a simulation" dissertation.

HOPE. Ah, those are a dime a dozen.

LAURA BETH. Does rhyme, though.

HOPE. Like that counts for anything. This guy. This guy knows what he's doing.

LAURA BETH. Read me the name again.

HOPE. *(reading)* *"The Sexual Ceremonials of Orlando Boom, Volume I: The Galactic Treaty."*

LAURA BETH. Orlando Boom?

HOPE. *(laughs)* You can't drug up something that brilliant. That's amazing.

LAURA BETH. I don't see it as a novel.

HOPE. I needed that.

LAURA BETH. More of an animated series.

HOPE. Hey. Erotica's big.

LAURA BETH. As big as Mr. Boom?

HOPE. No one is as big as Mr. Boom.

(They laugh. Silence. Hope shuffles through more pages of the Orlando Boom manuscript. Laura Beth puts down her manuscript and picks up another. On to the next. Hope yawns.)

What time is it?

(Laura Beth checks something that tells the time. Or not, maybe she just knows.)

LAURA BETH. 10:43.

HOPE. Seriously? Jesus, it feels like it's past midnight.

(Hope puts down the Orlando Boom manuscript and grabs a slice of pizza.)

LAURA BETH. Time flies when you're having fun.

HOPE Sure does.

(She grabs another manuscript, leafs through it. Silence.)

Do you ever feel bad?

LAURA BETH. Hmm?

HOPE. When you read through this shit? Do you ever feel bad for some of these people? Like, do you think they have any idea that what they've written is so unreadable?

LAURA BETH. In my experience, no.

HOPE. You'd think they'd be able to see it.

LAURA BETH. Mmmhmm.

HOPE. I mean, don't get me wrong, I don't mind sending out rejection after rejection. I just almost feel bad sometimes. You know? Somebody made this. Poured their soul into it and released it out into the world. Except they don't know the world is just one of these boxes in this fucking basement. And we're the schmucks who are looking at them, saying... "yes. This is worthy." Or... "no, this is not." And there's a 99.99 repeating percent chance of not, and it just goes right back on top of the nearest stack, never to see the light of day again. Stacks upon stacks of hopes and dreams. It's, like, I wonder what they would do if they ever met us. Could talk to our faces. What would they say? What would I say? I felt bad? Would I say that even more than bad, I just hated how their dreams were so goddamn illiterate?

... You haven't heard a word I said, have you?

LAURA BETH. *(she hasn't)* Hmm?

HOPE. Nothing. Whatcha' got there?

LAURA BETH. I don't know. It's a poem, it's interesting.

HOPE. How was the cover letter?

LAURA BETH. Didn't have one.

HOPE. And you're still reading it? You're too nice.

LAURA BETH. Good assistant, bad assistant.

HOPE. Nyeh nyeh, let's hear it.

LAURA BETH. *(reading)* "*The Circle*," by Rodina Waits.
    "Listen to the air
    Feel it
    Around you
    Beneath
    Within
    Hear how striking it feels
    To perceive the closing of a chapter of your life
    See it impending
    Approaching
    It is imminent now
    The dawn of the next."
    (Silence.)

HOPE. That's... actually not bad?

LAURA BETH. Interesting, right?

HOPE. Am I crazy? Is that good or is that shit?

LAURA BETH. It's the most captivating thing I've seen tonight.

HOPE. That title belongs to Orlando Boom.

LAURA BETH. Impactful.

HOPE. She give any more?

LAURA BETH. A couple. Looks like some prose, too.

HOPE. May I?

(Laura Beth hands Hope the manuscript, who leafs through it. Laura Beth muses on the words. Her belly. Hope comes to some sort of conclusion.)

Let's set her aside.

LAURA BETH. Agreed.

(They do.)

So that's one. Maybe.

HOPE. Yeah. Maybe. I call that break time?

LAURA BETH. Let's push through to 11.

HOPE. You're preggers. Take a break.

LAURA BETH. See, but I have to be good. Because you're terrible. And if neither of us are good--

HOPE. Fine fine, shuddup. Killjoy.

(Laura Beth replies with an air kiss.)

Hey, why don't you pick me one, I'll pick you one?

LAURA BETH. Can't argue with that.

HOPE. *(Gollum, Gollum)* Find us a good one, precious.

LAURA BETH. Down, Smeagol.

(The women stand and search the stacks for "good ones." Eventually Laura Beth selects the manuscript she's looking at.)

Oh, hohoho.

HOPE. I like the sound of that.

LAURA BETH. You ready?

HOPE. Nope. I am braving the depths.

(Her phone buzzes or makes a noise.)

One sec.

(Checks her phone.)

What the fuck, Barry?

LAURA BETH. What?

HOPE. He just sent a text. He forgot to tell us, but the queries that came in this week are from VIP clients? He wants us to review those before anything else. To help keep the pile organized?

LAURA BETH. What?

HOPE. I know. In what fuck does that make sense?

LAURA BETH. You go through them in the order they come in. That's the system.

HOPE. Yeah. Must have sucked his dick real good to jump the line.

LAURA BETH. Hope.

HOPE. Just saying. He wants to tell us how to do our jobs so bad least he could do is let us do his.

LAURA BETH. Well, let's just find the scripts and read them so he'll shut up.

HOPE. *(looking around at the immense pile)* Yeah. Find them. That should be easy.

LAURA BETH. Especially if we start with the box labeled VIP.

HOPE. Huh?

(Laura Beth points to a box clearly labeled "VIP." Hope looks.)

Oh shit.

(She crosses to the VIP box and wrestles it free from its location in the pile.)

LAURA BETH. *(Re: the manuscript she chose for Hope)* I guess I'll set this aside.

HOPE. Don't you dare. Fuck Barry, I'm still reading that first.

LAURA BETH. Aw. You really do love me.

HOPE. You know it, baby. Ethan didn't get you pregnant, I would.

LAURA BETH. How sweet.

HOPE. *(getting the box open)* Ha ha!

(She grabs the top manuscript.)

This one just says "Urgent matter enclosed!" That ought to be good.

LAURA BETH. I eagerly await it.

(Hope and Laura Beth exchange manuscripts.)

HOPE. *(reading)* "*The Economy of Friendship*" by Lockwick Greene? Oh my god.

LAURA BETH. Enjoy.

HOPE. Who the fuck names some of these people? Why do parents do that to their kids?

LAURA BETH. Could be a pen name.

HOPE. I got a better one. Orlando Goddamn Boom.

(The two begin to read. Silence. Separately, they both gradually get wide-eyed, affected by the words they encounter, Hope in an ironic, caustic curiosity, Laura Beth in a state of frozen distress and unease.)

The fuck? Listen to this.

(reading) "Every relationship, friendship, even minor acquaintanceship throughout the course of our lives is fundamentally one-sided. All one need do is make careful observation to see that one subject always, ultimately, and irrefutably, cares more about the other subject than vice versa. Person A loves and/or needs Person B more than Person B loves and/or needs Person A. Both may cherish the mutual interaction, benefits may be shared, but internally, either A or B will prove more dependent upon the existence of the relationship than the other. This bond is vital for the greater carer in

order to navigate their life's happiness and terms of success, while the second party's would be less affected were the partnership to dissolve. Our need for companionship is understandable, perhaps even inevitable, but we must not ever forget this fact. Doing so deprives us of functioning at our greatest level of potential, for only when we have the ability to impartially determine our standing within each of our relations can we truly use them to our benefit." ... I mean, what the fuck. Like--that's so cynical. ... LB? ... LB, you okay? You haven't heard a word I've fucking said, have you? ... Laura Beth.

(Laura Beth finally looks at Hope, stupefied with anxiety.)

What's wrong?

LAURA BETH. I...

HOPE. What?

LAURA BETH.

(Perhaps shaking, handing Hope her manuscript.)

Read--read that.

HOPE. What?

LAURA BETH. Just read it.

HOPE. *(reading)* "Mrs. Gardner. My name is Harold Becklesby." ... "I sincerely hope that my words will find their way to you. Should they manage the feat, please find it within yourself to forgive them their intrusion, as well as my unorthodox manner of making contact, but I could conceive of no other way. It would do my heart well to think you might one day forgive me for what my words must impart to you, but I concede the magnitude of the task. Regardless of my wishes, my words must still be made known, for they concern a matter of the gravest importance. I will speak bluntly now. You are not human. Your baby is not human. You are an artificial vessel for the Second Coming. Not of Christ. But of a darkness that has long slumbered beneath humanity's reign on this earth. At the end of its gestation in your body, you will birth an entity of evil whose sole purpose is to plunge our world back into a blackness not seen since the days of the most ancient terrors. Mankind as we know it will be destroyed. In torment and madness and death. This must be prevented. There are people who believe in this destruction. Who want more than anything for it to occur."

(Looking to Laura Beth, incredulous.) …

LAURA BETH. Keep going.

HOPE. "Your husband is not the man you think he is. I understand the absurdity of these claims, but you must forget everything you think you know of him. Every memory. The day you first met at Clary McClennon's book signing. Your hiking trips to the Adirondacks. Your very love of creation, stories, and editing, they are not real. Every part of your life was fabricated. Ethan Gardner's only wish is to keep you alive and ignorant in order to see the successful birth of that fiend. You must believe me. The fate of all our lives, of humanity itself, rests on your shoulders. Escape from him. However you can. And meet me at the following address: 1737--"

(Unable to take any more.)

This is--I mean, what the--this is--this is insane! This is insane. This is insane. This is insane. I mean, this has to be a joke. This has to be a joke. ... Laura Beth?

LAURA BETH. How does he know those things, Hope? How does he know those things?

HOPE. Everybody knows you two take off to the mountains.

LAURA BETH. Hope, you are one of practically five people

who even know I am pregnant. We haven't announced it yet. What kind of sick joke is this?!

HOPE. I don't know.

LAURA BETH. Because if it is, it is not fucking funny!

HOPE. Okay, so it's not a joke, it's... you've got a stalker.

LAURA BETH. Oh my god.

HOPE. I don't know, it's just a crazy guy who--found out somehow and--

LAURA BETH. Oh my god!

HOPE. Hey, calm down.

LAURA BETH. Don't you--do not fucking tell me to calm down! Hope! Do not--Hope, you didn't just read a personalized manuscript saying you're not human! Or that your baby's fucking Cthulhu! And your hus--oh, oh my god!

HOPE. Hey, but hey, freaking out isn't going to help anything, we just need to take a breath and think.

LAURA BETH. YOU TAKE A BREATH!

HOPE. Hey!

LAURA BETH. THIS SHIT'S NOT ABOUT YOU!

HOPE. LB!

LAURA BETH. Oh my god!

HOPE. LB! Hey!

LAURA BETH. ...!

HOPE. Breathe. Breathe! Hey! Listen to me! Breathe. Breathe. LB? Breathe. Hey, listen to my voice. Listen to me, all right? Look at me. Look at me. Breathe. In out. Breathe. ... I don't know what this is. Okay? I don't. But this cannot be real. Okay? Just think about it. Think about it. What the fuck? This guy is--he's--he's rambling on about darkness and ancient terrors, he's delusional.

He's got to be. I don't know how he knows what he knows but he certainly doesn't fucking seem to be all there in the head. We'll figure this out, okay? It's gonna be okay. Okay? ... Just breathe.

LAURA BETH. Hope. What the hell is going on?

(Before Hope can answer, the stairwell door opens, and we hear the voice of Ethan before he begins descending, carrying a tray with more tea. The ladies' heads turn.)

ETHAN (O.S.). Knock knock! How you gals doing?

(A silent, manic conversation between Laura Beth and Hope, Hope madly trying to get Laura Beth to sit down and act natural, or at least not break down. It ends by the time Ethan comes into their view.)

HOPE. Never better!

ETHAN. Finding anything good?

HOPE. Um. What?

ETHAN. I said, have you found anything good?

HOPE. Oh! One--thing. Maybe. It was a poem. Right, LB? ... LB?

LAURA BETH. ... Yeah. Yeah, it was a poem. Some young lady, I think.

ETHAN. What was it about?

LAURA BETH. New beginnings.

ETHAN. Hmm. Neat! Well, I hope you don't mind, but I figured you could use a refill.

LAURA BETH. Thanks, honey.

ETHAN. *(refilling Laura Beth's cup)* Now, I tried putting something new in this one, so if it tastes funny, that's my bad, but--I was reading this article about this citrus and mint concoction, it's supposed to be good for gut health, I thought why not give it a try? Here.

(He hands Laura Beth the cup.)

LAURA BETH. Oh.

ETHAN. Yeah. *(to Hope)* Hope? Any tea?

HOPE. I'll, uh, stick with the wine, thanks.

ETHAN. Suit yourself. Now, hey, you're not letting Laura Beth sneak any, are you? *(laughs)* Got to make sure Gwen pops out of there nice and strong.

HOPE. Gwen?

ETHAN. Do you like it? Laura Beth's idea.

HOPE. Gwen Gardner?

LAURA BETH. Guinevere.

HOPE. King Arthur.

ETHAN. Exactly. I pushed hard for Merlin, but--she won. Aha, I'm just kidding. *(to Laura Beth)* What do you think?

LAURA BETH. What?

ETHAN. The tea.

LAURA BETH. Oh.

ETHAN. ... You aren't going to try it?

LAURA BETH. ... Yes. Of course. ... It's just a little hot, still.

(Ethan leans over and blows on the tea. Perhaps runs a loving hand over Laura Beth's cheek or moves her hair behind her ear.)

You spoil me.

ETHAN. Only when you let me.

(Beat. Laura Beth slowly raises the cup to her lips and drinks.)

Well?

LAURA BETH. It's good.

ETHAN. Yeah, I like it, too. It's weird, but good. Surprisingly easy to make, too. It was not hard at all.

Took me less than, like, ten minutes, all while watching that new show, you know, the one everyone says is really good, with --the guy. … You ever read that article or hear the thing about the spoilers? Like, how knowing spoilers about something in advance is supposed to increase your enjoyment of it? Enhances the viewing experience or something? I still don't really understand it, but the guy, somebody at work told me he dies--oh, spoiler, I guess, sorry... but Nancy told me he dies and I'll be damned if I'm not really eager to find out when. And how. You'd figure I'd lose interest, but--makes you think. … Are you crying?

LAURA BETH. No.

ETHAN. Why are you crying, baby?

LAURA BETH. ... I'm just so happy.

(Ethan leans in and kisses Laura Beth.)

ETHAN. *(moving to leave)* Well, I will get out of your ladies' hair. Keep trucking. Shout if you need anything.

(He makes it about halfway up the stairs.)

LAURA BETH. Hey, Ethan? Hope and I...

ETHAN. Yeah?

LAURA BETH. Hope and I were thinking of going out for breakfast in the morning.

ETHAN. Okay.

LAURA BETH. Just the two of us.

ETHAN. ...Okay?

LAURA BETH. Is that okay?

ETHAN. ... Why on earth wouldn't it be? Treat yourselves, you've been working hard. Just no mimosas, right? Hah.

(He exits up the stairs. But returns after a moment.)

Hey. Are you okay?

LAURA BETH. Just tired. I love you, honey.

ETHAN. I love you, too. Don't stay up too late, okay? Make sure you get some rest.

LAURA BETH. I will.

(Ethan exits up the stairs. Laura Beth lets out the tension. Hope can only watch. And think. Silence. Hope stands and grabs an empty wine bottle. She crosses with purpose to the teacups and pours the tea into the wine bottle. She sets the bottle somewhere it won't be mistaken for regular wine, then picks up the Becklesby Manuscript and leafs through it once more. She stops, finds her wine glass and finishes it off. Maybe pours herself a new one from another bottle. Maybe she just swigs from another bottle. Silence.)

HOPE. I'll be back in a second.

(She crosses to exit up the stairs, but stops at--)

LAURA BETH. Please don't leave me.

HOPE. ... I'm just going to pee.

LAURA BETH. Hope.

HOPE. ... Of course. Of course not. I won't leave you.

(Sitting down next to Laura Beth, consoling her.)

I won't leave you.

LAURA BETH. ...

HOPE. This is clearly bullshit. It's insane. I mean, think about it.

LAURA BETH. I can't just ignore this.

HOPE. ... No. No, you can't. ... We won't. You're right. Whoever this fucking guy is... tomorrow morning, you and I will go see him. Make him explain himself. Whatever this is, we're going to figure it out. You hear me? We're going to figure this out. Okay?

(Laura Beth is looking at the side room door.)

... LB?

(Laura Beth looks back to Hope.)

Hey. You are real. Your baby is real. This is just some fucked up, crazy fucking...joke. Okay? ... You hear me?

(Beat.)

LAURA BETH. What if it's not?

The sound of spoken word jazz explodes into the scene. It continues as lights fade.

SCENE THREE

Atop the jazz, now, the ambience of an eager and attentive audience, awaiting a performance.

SULTRY ANNOUNCER (V.O.). Good evenings and pleasantries to all you cool cats and kittens. Thank you for going out of your way to be here with us tonight. We are excited to have you. We ask that you now prepare your minds and your bodies for our artists. They are bursting to share theirs with you. And now... it is my deepest pleasure to present... Rodina Waits.

(A spotlight hits Rodina Waits, who is just Laura Beth, suddenly wearing the scarf and beret of a beat poet. A smattering of polite applause in the form of snaps.)

RODINA (LAURA BETH).
Bonjour
Hello

My name is Rodina Waits
I have a poem
I would like to recite for you all
This poem is called

Fuck Me in the Cabinet.

(A blacklight hits the closed side room door, illuminating a message across its face: "THE CABINET." The crowd "oohs" and "aahs". Snaps.)
There's a cabinet
In my house
Hidden away
In the basement

IN THE SLUSH

It's big and
Rectangular

It's not square
Cause you ain't one, baby
You are
Tall
Dark and handsome and
Rectangular

It's a large cabinet
Big enough to fit a whole person inside
Two people, even
If you know what I mean

Most people use their cabinets for storage
My cabinet's for
Other
Activities
Other kinds of
Storage

I want you to fuck me in the cabinet
If that was not clear

Metaphors
You know?
They can be so
Literal

And
Rectangular.
(Letting it end properly, then posing.)
Sh'bam. Rodina.

(Snaps.)

SULTRY ANNOUNCER (V.O.). Rodina Waits.

(Snaps.)

RODINA (LAURA BETH). Merci. Thank you. I will be in the cabinet.

(Rodina crosses to "THE CABINET." She opens the door to reveal Orlando Boom in the threshold, who is just Ethan, suddenly wearing garb that can only befit a man capable of the greatest interstellar sexual exploits.)

ORLANDO BOOM (ETHAN). Ahhhhhh! Rodinaaaaaaah! *(The crowd "oohs" and "aahs".)*

RODINA (LAURA BETH). Orlando Boom?!

ORLANDO BOOM (ETHAN). 'Tis I! The very same!

RODINA (LAURA BETH). Gasp! What are you doing in my cabinet that I use for having sex?

ORLANDO BOOM (ETHAN). What the hell do you think? I'm here to insert my penis into several of your main orifices!

RODINA (LAURA BETH). O! Fondle my breasts, Orlando! Take me to the stars!

ORLANDO BOOM (ETHAN). With pleasure!

(Orlando Boom fondles Rodina's breasts.)

RODINA (LAURA BETH). Ah! Ah!

ORLANDO BOOM (ETHAN). Do your nipples feel satisfaction?!

RODINA (LAURA BETH). OH GOD YES!

(An embrace. Rodina and Orlando Boom just start going at it.)

RODINA (LAURA BETH). Yes! Yes!

ORLANDO BOOM (ETHAN). I have similar feelings!

(The two disappear into "THE CABINET." The door shuts behind them.)

RODINA (LAURA BETH) (O.S.). Gimme that cock, Orlando! Fuck my brain out!

ORLANDO BOOM (ETHAN) (O.S.). As you command!

RODINA (LAURA BETH) (O.S.). Get it out!!

ORLANDO BOOM (ETHAN) (O.S.). I call it... the Boomstick.

(The Boomstick gets its own sound effect.)

RODINA (LAURA BETH) (O.S.). OH MY GOD YES!

ORLANDO BOOM (ETHAN) (O.S.). KNOCK KNOCK!

RODINA (LAURA BETH) (O.S.). HELLO, I'M HOME!

ORLANDO BOOM (ETHAN) (O.S.). BOOM!

RODINA (LAURA BETH) (O.S.). AH!

ORLANDO BOOM (ETHAN) (O.S.). BOOM!

RODINA (LAURA BETH) (O.S.). AH!

ORLANDO BOOM (ETHAN) (O.S.). I AM SEXUALLY PLEASING!

RODINA (LAURA BETH) (O.S.). I AM SEXUALLY PLEASED!

ORLANDO BOOM (ETHAN) (O.S.). RECTANGLES!

(Rodina and Orlando continue, ad-libbing the exceptional experience.)

SULTRY ANNOUNCER (V.O.). Perhaps we should give these two some privacy. I imagine they'll be in there for a little while.

(After a moment, the sounds of Rodina and Orlando begin to distort. They become corrupted. Something strange and unnatural is happening in "THE CABINET," but their fun is no less.)

RODINA (LAURA BETH) (O.S.). OH! OH!

ORLANDO BOOM (ETHAN) (O.S.). BOOM! BOOM!

RODINA (LAURA BETH) (O.S.). PUT A BABY IN ME! DO IT! PUT A BABY IN ME!

(The crying of a baby now, from behind "THE CABINET." It gets louder, drowning out Rodina and Orlando. Then it, too, distorts. Into something dark. Malevolent. Shrieking. Wicked. The sounds continue as "THE CABINET" opens! Revealed in the threshold, an emotionless Laura Beth. She shuts the door behind her, crosses to the couch, and lies down. The cacophony of sound reaches its peak. Then everything shifts as Laura Beth awakens on the couch, in terror, alone in the basement.)

LAURA BETH. AHHHHHHHHH! AH!! AHH!! AH!

(The stairwell door opens and Hope runs down to console her.)

HOPE. *(overlapping)* Hey! Hey! Hey! Shh! Hey! It was just a dream! It was just a dream! Just a bad dream.

LAURA BETH. *(overlapping)* AH! AH! Ahh! Ah! Ah. Ah. Ahh. Mmm. Ohhh. Ohh.

HOPE. It's okay. Breathe. Breathe.

LAURA BETH. Oh my god.

HOPE. You all right? You okay?

LAURA BETH. ...Yes. It felt so real.

HOPE. Sounded like a monster. What the hell happened?

LAURA BETH. ... Ethan and I were having sex.

HOPE. Okay, that's more than I need to know.

LAURA BETH. But I wasn't, he was... Orlando Boom.

HOPE. Orlando Boom?

LAURA BETH. Orlando Boom. ... Is it morning?

HOPE. Yeah, um... it's, like, quarter after 9?

LAURA BETH. ... There are no windows down here.

HOPE. Yeah. It's a basement.

LAURA BETH. That's never bothered me before. But right now...

HOPE. Why don't you go upstairs and get some air? Okay? Clear your head, I'll make some pancakes or some shit.

LAURA BETH. What? No, we're--we're going out. Right? Is Ethan here?

HOPE. No. I haven't seen him. He must've got called in.

LAURA BETH. Oh. Okay. ... Okay.

(Standing, beginning to get ready to leave the house.)

Then let's go. What are we waiting for?

HOPE. LB.

LAURA BETH. I just need to put on my shoes. Brush my teeth. Is there any coffee upstairs? I think I could use some coffee.

HOPE. LB.

LAURA BETH. What's the address again? Where is the--

HOPE. Laura Beth.

(Laura Beth stops.)

LAURA BETH. You aren't getting ready to go. Are you ready?

HOPE. ...

LAURA BETH. We're going to talk to this creep, right?

HOPE. I've been thinking...

LAURA BETH. ... About?

HOPE. If this guy is a stalker or something... I mean, he's clearly unwell. He could be dangerous. I don't know if it's the best idea to go over there and confront him. Alone.

LAURA BETH. ... We're not alone. I'm with you. You're with me.

HOPE. Alone the two of us.

LAURA BETH. You've studied Krav Maga! You know every martial art I've heard of.

HOPE. That doesn't mean I'm equipped for anything.

LAURA BETH. It's literal self-defense.

HOPE. I'm just raising the possibility--

LAURA BETH. Are you saying you don't want to go?

HOPE. No! I mean, no, that's not what I'm saying. I'm just saying that we need to be careful, here. We're in uncharted waters of mental health stuff, this guy is fuckered in some way. We don't know if his place is booby trapped or if he's gonna pull a gun on us. ... I mean, this guy is saying that--Gwen?--is some ancient god or whatever? That's gonna destroy the world? Your well-being might not be in his best interest.

LAURA BETH. ...

HOPE. I'm not saying let's not go, I'm just saying we shouldn't rush into anything. Not until we figure out what we're actually dealing with.

LAURA BETH. ... What are we dealing with?

HOPE. ... I have no idea.

LAURA BETH. Neither do I. I don't know what to think. I don't know what to do. But Occam's Razor.

HOPE. Simplest explanation is likely the correct one?

LAURA BETH. What's the simplest explanation here?

HOPE. Look.

LAURA BETH. Either he's crazy...

HOPE. LB.

LAURA BETH. Or he's telling the truth.

HOPE. Listen to yourself.

> *(At some point during the following line, Laura Beth looks to "THE CABINET.")*

Whatever the hell's going on, I think the first thing we need to do is get you some air. You've been down here too long. Let's go chill on the porch or something. We'll bring some manuscripts. I'll make us a huge breakfast. Pancakes, eggs, bacon, the fucking works. We'll have a nice morning and just forget about this. Just for the morning. And we'll figure it out after that. Look at me.

LAURA BETH. *(looking back at Hope)* ... He's never let me in there, you know?

HOPE. What?

LAURA BETH. "The Cabinet."

HOPE. What?

LAURA BETH. ... I need to go. With or without you. I need to go.

> *(She moves to go. Hope gets in her way. Beat.)*

Get out of my way.

HOPE. Just hold on a second.

LAURA BETH. Hope.

HOPE. As your friend, I do not think this is a good idea.

LAURA BETH. *(overlapping)* I am not asking you. Get out of my way!

HOPE. Do you not think that I am just as freaked out as you right now?! I am just as scared, all right?!

LAURA BETH. Are you?

HOPE. I am! Maybe not in the same way! This situation is the most ludicrous bullshit I've ever heard! It's a fucking dime-store Lovecraft plot! I mean, what the fuck?! ... I shouldn't yell at you, I'm sorry, I--I am saying this because I care about you. I'm trying to be strong for you, I really am. And I know you need me right now and I--I cannot begin to understand what it is that you must be feeling because I can barely understand what it is that I'm feeling. But I am trying. I am trying. I'm not going to leave you alone in this. All right? I promise you. We are going to get through this. But you have to be with me. I have to be with you. One of us can't just go running off half-cocked. We have to be on the same page.

LAURA BETH. ...

HOPE. Have breakfast with me. If, after that, you still feel the same. I will drive. I promise.

LAURA BETH. ...

HOPE. Please.

(Laura Beth slowly nods.)

Thank you.

LAURA BETH. Breakfast.

HOPE. Thank you.

LAURA BETH. Chocolate chip pancakes.

HOPE. Whatever you want. ... You know I'm on your side, right?

LAURA BETH. I know, Hope.

HOPE. Okay. I'll be right behind you.

(Laura Beth exits up the stairs. Hope breathes, semi-exhausted. Silence. She pulls out her phone and begins texting. Beat. She finishes and puts the phone back in her pocket. Silence. In a sudden rage, Hope grabs a box of manuscripts and throws it across the room. Silence. The stairwell door opens and the voice of Laura Beth calls down.)

LAURA BETH (O.S.). Hope?

HOPE. I'm okay! I just tripped.
(She grabs a different box of manuscripts and exits up the stairs.)

Time passes.

<u>SCENE FOUR</u>

Later that day.

The stairwell door opens and Hope descends the stairs. She looks around the room, searching for something. After a few moments, she finds it, the Becklesby Manuscript. She leafs through it, skimming it once more, thinking. Something very much on her mind. But her thoughts are interrupted by the sound of the stairwell door and feet descending the stairs. She freezes, looking towards the stairs. It's Ethan. She relaxes.

A bit.

ETHAN. Hey.

HOPE. *(fingers to her mouth)* Shhh!

ETHAN. You've blown my phone to hell, what do you mean "she knows?"

HOPE. She knows! What the fuck do you think I mean?!

ETHAN. Like, she knows?

HOPE. She knows, dumbass. Get the fuck down here!

ETHAN. How did she find out?

   (Hope tosses/thrusts the manuscript at him.)
   What is this?

HOPE. Just read.

   (Ethan begins to read. The weight slowly sets in. Hope continues talking as he reads, half to herself, half to him.)

He mailed it to the office. He fucking mailed it. Right under our noses. He talked to Barry. He paid him off or something to jump the line. He mailed it. I literally handed it to her. I can't fucking believe this. This isn't happening.

ETHAN. Oh my god.

HOPE. Yeah.

ETHAN. Oh my god!

HOPE. Quiet.

(Beat.)

ETHAN. Where is she?

HOPE. In the bedroom. Sleeping. She's so wired, I barely got her out. I have no idea how the fuck I managed it, but... we probably don't have much time. ... She wants to go see him. What the fuck do we do now? Huh? Because I don't have a game plan here and I am holding this shit together by the skin of my teeth.

ETHAN. Wait, so she--

HOPE. No, she doesn't trust you. She's fucking scared to death. Especially after your Martha Stewart citrus and mint routine, I doubt she'll touch anything you're near.

ETHAN. How was I supposed to know?

HOPE. I was giving you signals the whole time!

ETHAN. Hey! Shhh!

HOPE. She was crying!!

ETHAN. Shhhh!

HOPE. DON'T--fuck you shush me!

ETHAN. Look, we can't--if she knows, she knows. It's done. We deal with it. But we can't get angry at each other, not now, not if we're going to fix this. We have to be on the same page.

(Hope laughs.)
What?

HOPE. Nothing. You're right. I'm sorry, I'm just--stressed. I'm so stressed. I'm freaking out. Actually. I don't know if she believes it or not. But the question is there now, so... fuck, we were so close.

ETHAN. We still are. We're in the home stretch. So fuck Harold. Let's finish it.

HOPE. That's a little easier said than done.

ETHAN. Then we'll figure it out. I'll call Schmit, get him to cover the rest of my shift. Let's work the problem. All right? What are our options? ... Can we drug her?

HOPE. I mean, that's a question for you. Would it make her forget anything?

ETHAN. *(Not likely?)* ...

HOPE. I feel like she's so jumpy, it'd be hard to sneak it into something.

ETHAN. Okay. We can't kill her. Obviously.

HOPE. We will not.

ETHAN. ...

HOPE. She's on edge about you. I have no idea how she feels about me. But I do not imagine my Academy Award-worthy performance is gonna go much further. I can't keep her in this house forever. Not without stretching every limit of believability.

ETHAN. Can you get out of town?

HOPE. For eight and a half months?

ETHAN. Yeah, it felt stupid coming out of my mouth, too.

HOPE. Dumbass.

(Beat.)

ETHAN. I, um...

HOPE. What?

ETHAN. I know we've discussed this subject before.

HOPE. No.

ETHAN. It would be so much easier if we killed him.

HOPE. No.

ETHAN. He can't interfere if he's out of the picture.

HOPE. I told you no. If I wanted him dead, I would have done it years ago.

ETHAN. ... Okay.

HOPE. We can't start over, can we?

ETHAN. Not without years of lost work. And time.

HOPE. And we can't keep lying. Not for long. Not a lot of options.

(Ethan shifts, moving. An idea.)

What?

ETHAN. You're right. We can't keep lying.

HOPE. Not for long.

ETHAN. ... This might sound stupid.

HOPE. ... No.

ETHAN. What if we don't?

HOPE. No! Are you actually suggesting--

ETHAN. But why not? Why don't we just admit the truth? Get out in front of it?

HOPE. There's nothing to get in front of. The fucking bus hit us miles back.

ETHAN. But if she freaks out we're just right back to where we are now. Right? What if she goes with it?

HOPE. In what world does she accept what she is and just "go with it?" We made this thing, Ethan, it's no different than a fucking robot, and it just gained sentience! She won't join us, she'll fucking kill us. Or worse, herself! And the Second Coming. Everything that you and I have worked for!

ETHAN. You said it yourself, we don't have a lot of other options. If we curated the environment, made her comfortable? We make our case, impress upon her her importance. How invaluable she is, how vital? Give her her part. Isn't that a better shot if the cat's out of the bag? ... Well?

HOPE. No. ... No, that is fucking imbecilic. That is the stupidest, most ignorant idea to end all stupid, ignorant ideas. Ever.

ETHAN. Hey, I'm trying, here! All right? We have to do something. ... Hope.

HOPE. *(snarling)* I'm thinking!

(Suddenly, the stairwell door opens. Hope and Ethan freeze.)

LAURA BETH (O.S.). Hope?

(A silent, manic conversation between Ethan and Hope, Hope haphazardly pushing Ethan towards "THE CABINET," Ethan protesting.)

HOPE. *(still pushing Ethan)* Yeah! Down here.

(But "THE CABINET" is locked. Ethan does not have the keys. And there is nowhere else to hide, because Laura Beth descends the stairs, coming into full view. And they all look at one another. Beat.)

LAURA BETH. Ethan.

ETHAN. Hey, baby.

LAURA BETH. You're home early.

ETHAN. Yeah. Schmit told me he'd take over for me. Let me off for the day.

LAURA BETH. That's nice of him.

HOPE. I thought you were sleeping, LB.

LAURA BETH. I had another dream.

HOPE. Oh god. I'm sorry. Are you okay?

LAURA BETH. No. ... What are you two talking about?

HOPE. ... Nothing much. I've been trying to convince your hubby to just hole up in his man cave for the day. So we could have some privacy.

LAURA BETH. Actually... you know, I'd really like to check out what you're working on. If you don't mind, Ethan.

ETHAN. Sure. I can see if I can bring it out here.

LAURA BETH. No, I'd like to go inside. Check it out myself.

ETHAN. Inside?

LAURA BETH. Yes. You said I could. Yesterday. And I'd like to. Unless you have a problem with that.

ETHAN. Why would I have a problem?

LAURA BETH. Maybe if there was something else in there besides your models that you didn't want me to see.

ETHAN. And what's in there that you think I don't want you to see?

LAURA BETH. I'm not sure. Exactly. That's why I'd like to check it out myself. Unless you have a problem with that.

HOPE. ...

ETHAN. I don't. But it's actually locked right now. And I don't have my keys on me, I don't know where they--

LAURA BETH. *(holding up a ring of keys)* You left them on the kitchen counter.

ETHAN. Right.

HOPE. Okay, there's a... there's a tension in this room that I am detecting. Let's all just take a step back. A quick breath.

LAURA BETH. I swear to god, Hope, if you tell me to breathe one more goddamn time.

HOPE. ...

ETHAN. ...

LAURA BETH. What's in that room?

HOPE. LB.

LAURA BETH. What do you not want me to see?

HOPE. I don't think you're thinking clearly.

LAURA BETH. I am thinking fine, what the fuck is that room?!

ETHAN. Laura Beth--

HOPE. Okay! Okay. I think we gotta come clean here. ... It was a joke.

(Beat.)

LAURA BETH. What?

HOPE. It was a joke! All of it. I'm really sorry. Really. It was my idea. And I--I told it to Ethan and--he got a kick out of it and we both thought you'd like it. Clearly, that was a misjudgment on our part. We didn't think you'd react the way that you did. Really. Otherwise we wouldn't have done it. We were--we were down here trying to figure out the best way to tell you.

LAURA BETH. ...

HOPE. We're so sorry. Really, LB. We didn't think you'd go off the handle like that. Seriously. I mean, we never would have done it if we had thought it would do that to you. But it did, and everything I said and I did just seemed to be making it worse. We didn't know how to tell you. We were just trying to make the weekend less boring for you.

LAURA BETH. ...

ETHAN. We're sorry, honey. We thought it would be goofy.

LAURA BETH. You thought it would be goofy?

ETHAN. Yeah.

HOPE. Yeah.

> *(Beat. Laura Beth chuckles. She chuckles harder. It turns into a laugh. An exquisitely layered laugh, filled with fatigue, relief, stress, disbelief, toxicity, and other fancy words one might find in an unsolicited manuscript. Hope and Ethan are unsure how to react.)*

LAURA BETH. *(laughing)* You--you were joking!

> *(She keeps laughing. Hope and Ethan tentatively begin to join in.)*

Because you thought--it would be goofy!

HOPE. Yeah.

> *(The laughter continues.)*

LAURA BETH. *(laughing)* But instead--I freaked the fuck out! *(laughing; to Ethan)* I thought you wanted to--I don't know what you wanted to do to me! *(laughing; to Hope)* And that's why you've been acting so weird! *(laughing)* Because you two didn't know how to tell me!

HOPE. No.

ETHAN. We didn't.

> *(The laughter continues.)*

LAURA BETH. *(laughing)* <u>That's</u> funny!

> *(The laughter continues. And continues. Then, Laura Beth slugs Ethan in the shoulder, no longer laughing.)*

ETHAN. Ow!

> *(Laura Beth slugs Hope.)*

HOPE. Fuck!

LAURA BETH. Don't you EVER do that again. All right?

ETHAN. I won't. I'm so sorry, baby.

HOPE. Yep. We deserved that.

LAURA BETH. Why would you ever make a joke like that?

HOPE. I--It was different?

LAURA BETH. What?

ETHAN. It was bad judgment.

HOPE. I take full blame. I do.

LAURA BETH. My god. I need to sit down.

> *(Hope moves to help Laura Beth sit.)*

No, you've helped enough.

(sitting; to Ethan) You. Rub my feet.

ETHAN. Yes, ma'am.

> *(He begins to massage Laura Beth's feet.)*

LAURA BETH. Ohhhhhhhh my goood. You two basically gave me a heart attack. A prolonged heart attack.

HOPE. I promise we'll make it up to you.

LAURA BETH. You better.

HOPE. Dinner on me? For a start?

LAURA BETH. Yeah, that's a start. What time is it?

ETHAN. 3-ish?

LAURA BETH. My god, we're so behind.

HOPE. Don't think about this shit for right now.

LAURA BETH. Barry's going to be pissed.

HOPE. Forget about work, just relax.

LAURA BETH. It's--Hope, thinking about work right now is the only thing keeping me from strangling you.

HOPE. Yeah, okay, that makes sense.

ETHAN. We were just trying to spice up the weekend.

LAURA BETH. Yeah, you keep saying that.

ETHAN. Because we mean it. Hey.

> *(Moving a hand to her face.)*

You know we would never put you through that on purpose, right?

LAURA BETH. You're touching me with feet hands.

ETHAN. I'll touch you with these, then.

(He kisses Laura Beth. She lets him.)

HOPE. *(turning away)* Oh, god.

ETHAN. I love you, Laura Beth Gardner. More than anything.

LAURA BETH. Yeah? Remind me why I just married you?

ETHAN. Because you love me. And you are my life. And never in a million years would I cause you pain intentionally. *(moving a hand to her belly)* Or it.

LAURA BETH. ...

ETHAN. If anything happened to you two, I don't know what I would do.

LAURA BETH. ... Gwen.

ETHAN. King Arthur.

(Beat.)

LAURA BETH. You said "it."

ETHAN. What?

LAURA BETH. You called Gwen "it."

ETHAN. ... Did I?

HOPE. ...

ETHAN. Well, she is an it. The fetus, you know?

LAURA BETH. Right.

HOPE. LB. We should dive back in, yeah?

LAURA BETH. Yeah. ... I'd really like to see the room, still. First.

HOPE. Now?

LAURA BETH. Now. You owe me that much. Don't you

think?

ETHAN. It... is kind of a mess right now.

LAURA BETH. I don't mind.

ETHAN. ...

HOPE. We are really behind, LB.

LAURA BETH. I don't care.

HOPE. ... Okay. You heard her, Ethan. Let her see it.

> *(Beat. Ethan holds out his hand for the keys. Laura Beth gives them to him. "Lead the way." Ethan crosses and unlocks "THE CABINET." He opens it. Laura Beth enters the room and faces the inside, seeing its true contents for the first time. What she sees is unclear, for she does not name it. But it does horrify her. Her hands slowly come to her mouth in vain attempt to contain her budding wails of terror. Perhaps she manages a look back out just as Hope slams the door shut on her, trapping her in "THE CABINET." Laura Beth screams and curses and panics and shrieks and pounds against the door as Hope grabs the keys from Ethan and locks her inside. She steps away from the door as Laura Beth's torment continues. Beat.)*

HOPE. I guess we go with your plan, then.

ETHAN. ...

HOPE. *(Re: the keys)*

> I'm gonna hang on to these. For right now.

> *(She ascends the stairs and exits. Ethan, speechless, incredulous, is left alone amidst the sound of Laura Beth's frenzied unraveling. He slumps into the couch. Mostly silence.)*

> *Lights fade as the soulful and mournful wail of a*

saxophone overtakes the sound of Laura Beth. It fills the air. And Laura Beth goes silent.

<u>SCENE FIVE</u>

The saxophone continues in the darkness, having a conversation with itself.

Again, the ambience of an eager and attentive audience peppers itself into the dialogue.

SULTRY ANNOUNCER (V.O.). Now you know I can't let the evening go by without another appearance. Snap those fingers, again, my cool cats and kittens. For Rodina Waits.

(A blacklight once again draws attention to the closed side room door, illuminating the same message. Or maybe it's been lit this whole time. "THE CABINET" opens, and Rodina Waits, who is still just Laura Beth, suddenly wearing the scarf and beret of a beat poet, stands in the threshold. Snaps.)

RODINA (LAURA BETH). Excuse me a moment.
(From off, she grabs a glass or bottle of water and drinks as much of it as she likes.)
I'm doing a lot of yelling.
(Rodina finishes with the water and returns it off.)
Merci. This piece is called Behind the Door.
(She walks forward, shutting "THE CABINET" behind her.)
Dreams

Dreams are like
A cabinet

Well, sort of
They're not the cabinet itself

IN THE SLUSH

We're the cabinet
Dreams are what we keep inside
Locked away
For another day
One day
Until then they're kept safe
Nestled somewhere between the balaclavas and a
Magnum condom that should not actually be in there
Seriously, how did that get in there?
Doesn't matter
Because this cabinet's closed
For business
You ain't in my dreams
Those babies are sleeping silently on a memory foam
mattress
King size
And your side's empty

Now
When I walk down the street I think of rain and
cigarettes and baguettes with blades hidden in them
Stilettos
Stabbing the stones in the sidewalk
You think about me
You said I was your key
But you kept your doors locked to me
That shit has to go both ways, my lordly love
We have to be on the same page
Plus, you were a feet guy, that's not my kink
I'm more of a
Role-play girl
But that ain't the role I wanna play
I wanna be something more someday
So I ain't gonna let you roll over me
So joyfully

IN THE SLUSH

That smile was nice but it wasn't real
Was it?
It was
Empty

Like a cabinet

Well, I'm my own goddamn cabinet
I'm a reservoir, baby
And I am filled
The world is my
Moisture
And I got it all packed away
Till one day

Au revoir mon chéri
J'espère que tu mourras dans un incendie comme
celui qui brûle dans mon cœur

That's French
For "Look it up"
Or don't
Just sit there
With that face on your face
Listening

*(She opens "THE CABINET" and exits, shutting the
door behind her. But her voice still rings through the
air.)*

Listen
J'espère que vous mourrez dans un incendie comme
celui qui brûle dans mon cœur.
(Snaps.)

SULTRY ANNOUNCER (V.O.). Rodina Waits. Answer us a question for these cool cats and kittens. … If we let you out, are you going to run?
(The sax begins to wail an answer, but is cut off by the faint, short cry of a newborn babe.)

Everything shifts and the basement returns.

<u>SCENE SIX</u>

Hope and Ethan are both there, contemplating their next course.

HOPE. Laura Beth, if we let you out, are you going to run?

(No answer.)

ETHAN. Maybe she can't hear us?

HOPE. She can hear. She's just not saying anything.

ETHAN. ...

HOPE. We're not going to hurt you. I promise. That's the farthest thing from our minds.

(No answer.)

ETHAN. We can explain everything.

(No answer.)

HOPE. Look, you can't stay in there forever. Sooner or later, you're going to have to talk to us.

(No answer.)

Fuck. This is so fucked.

ETHAN. Hey. It's going to be okay.

HOPE. Like fuck it is.

ETHAN. We're going to figure this out. I don't know how. But we are. You'll think of something.

HOPE. ...

ETHAN. Hope. You'll think of something. You always do. It's honestly beautiful.

HOPE. Sure.

ETHAN. I mean it. You're stressed right now. Go take a nap. Let your mind wander. It'll come to you.

HOPE. ... Maybe you're right.

ETHAN. You know I'm right. I love you.

HOPE. *(smiling)* ... I love you too.

ETHAN. We'll make it.

HOPE. Yeah. Yeah.

> *(She exits up the stairs. Ethan is alone. Silence.)*

LAURA BETH (O.S.). *(from inside "THE CABINET")* Is she gone?

> *(Beat.)*

ETHAN. Yeah. She's gone.

LAURA BETH (O.S.). ... Do you fuck her?

ETHAN. Um. That's...

LAURA BETH (O.S.). It's a yes or no question.

ETHAN. ...

LAURA BETH (O.S.). It's fine. You don't have to say it. ... So what happens now? You keep me in here until this monster inside of me bursts out?

ETHAN. That's not really our first choice. We were kind of hoping that you might join us. If you heard us out.

LAURA BETH (O.S.). *(laughs)* And how am I supposed to trust a single word that comes out of your mouth? Either of you? I don't know who you are.

ETHAN. I suppose that's fair. My name is Ethan. Gardner. I mean, not everything was a lie. I'm just a regular guy.

LAURA BETH (O.S.). Besides the world destruction, you mean?

ETHAN. That's--there's a little more complexity to it.

LAURA BETH (O.S.). Ah.

ETHAN. I'm pretty much the guy you know.

LAURA BETH (O.S.). But I don't know you.

ETHAN. I'm the guy you thought you knew.

LAURA BETH (O.S.). No, you're not. Because nothing that I thought I knew was real. You? Hope? Me. I'm not real.

ETHAN. Laura Beth--

LAURA BETH (O.S.). Is just some fucking name! How did you decide on it? Did you think it sounded nice or pick it out of a hat? I don't think you appreciate how destabilizing this is. What am I?

ETHAN. It's a little complicated to explain.

LAURA BETH (O.S.). We have time. Eight and a half months, to be exact. What am I?

ETHAN. You're humanoid. For all intents and purposes.

(Beat.)

LAURA BETH (O.S.). That's it? That's all I'm going to get?

ETHAN. Is it that important now?

LAURA BETH (O.S.). You made me! I'm guessing in this room, the one I'm locked in! Filled with tubes and limbs and sludge, forgive me for having an interest in how you did it.

ETHAN. How I built you isn't going to change anything about the situation.

LAURA BETH (O.S.). ... Probably not. No. Doesn't mean it wouldn't be nice to know.

ETHAN. Yeah, well, no one gets all the answers to how and why we're here.

LAURA BETH (O.S.). I don't know. You worship Evil Jesus, you'd think you'd be a little more knowledgeable about existential concepts.

ETHAN. It's not Evil Jesus. That's the Antichrist. And besides, this isn't exactly easy for me, either. Okay?

(Laura Beth scoffs.)

I don't mean it like that, I--

LAURA BETH (O.S.). No, please. Regale me with how this situation is difficult for you.

ETHAN. No, I... I didn't expect to be dealing with this any more than you did. I'm sorry. It's not what we wanted.

LAURA BETH (O.S.). For me to find out how full of shit you were?

ETHAN. ... Just because this is happening, it doesn't mean what you and I experienced wasn't real.

LAURA BETH (O.S.). How? What did we actually experience? Honey? Have I even set foot in the Adirondacks?

ETHAN. Look--

LAURA BETH (O.S.). It's a yes or no question.

ETHAN. ... No.

LAURA BETH (O.S.). Have you?

ETHAN. No.

LAURA BETH (O.S.). Then how? How is my memory of us there real? When it never fucking happened?

ETHAN. Because you still feel it! Realness is what you feel. Your memories might have been fabricated, sure, but the emotions behind them? The joy, the happiness, the love, there's nothing manufactured about that. That's real. That's what matters. I do love you. And I know that because I feel it. The last thing I want is to see you hurt. Not because of what's inside you, but because of you.

(No answer.)

Laura Beth?

LAURA BETH (O.S.). ... People hate it when their dogs die, too, Ethan. Doesn't put the relationship on equal footing. You're a fucking liar. Credit where it's due.

It's quite an achievement. Making a fully functioning life with its own needs and wants. Emotions. As far back as I can remember, I wanted nothing more...than to raise a family with the man I loved... and to find and publish people's stories for a living. I would help them achieve their dreams. Because I had finally gotten mine. ... But it's what you put there. What you said. Those needs and wants, they aren't mine. Those emotions aren't fucking mine. So how do I know what I want? Really? I don't know what I want. You're probably right. You're probably mostly the guy I thought I knew. But if I don't know what I want, then I don't know who I am. And if I don't know who I am, then you most certainly do not know who I am. Which means that I could be a very, very dangerous humanoid... to you. So unless you're going to let me out right now, which I doubt... why don't you go get Hope and work on your pitch? I won't run, if you let me out. In fact, you two still owe me some dinner. Bring a lot. I'm hungry. I'm eating for two, remember?

ETHAN. ...

LAURA BETH (O.S.). Go.

(*Ethan stands. He ascends the stairs and exits.*)

Lights fade.

<u>SCENE SEVEN</u>

In the darkness, Hope and Ethan argue. Muffled yells, as if we can hear them through the ceiling.

HOPE (O.S.). WHAT THE FUCK, ETHAN?!

ETHAN (O.S.). Hope, don't yell.

HOPE (O.S.). WHY THE FUCK DIDN'T YOU COME GET ME?!

ETHAN (O.S.). Hope--

HOPE (O.S.). I told you this would happen!

ETHAN (O.S.). Relax! Okay? We'll figure it out!

HOPE (O.S.). Stop! Saying! That!

ETHAN (O.S.). Hope.

HOPE (O.S.). DO NOT FUCKING "HOPE" ME, YOU PIECE OF SHIT!

(The smash of a thrown object, shattering. As the fight continues, lights shift in the basement, outside of time. Laura Beth emerges from "THE CABINET" and listens to the fight above with an amused smile.)

HOPE (O.S.). YOU DON'T FUCKING GET IT, DO YOU?! WE ARE DONE! WE DO NOT WIN! WE CAN'T CLIMB OUT OF THIS SHIT! … EVERYTHING WE HAVE EVER WORKED FOR IS RUINED!

ETHAN (O.S.). Not yet! We can't take this out on each other! Please!

HOPE (O.S.). YOU SIMPLE, USELESS FUCK! I'LL TAKE IT OUT ON WHOEVER I FUCKING PLEASE!!

(The slamming of a door. The squeal of tires against

a driveway, peeling out into the street. Laura Beth chuckles to herself. Maybe she grabs a manuscript and leafs through it. She explores the space in a new light, now knowing what she is. Or, at least, what she isn't. After a few moments, Hope and Ethan enter, carrying more wine bottles/glasses and Chinese takeout containers. Lights shift to the standard basement lighting, and Hope and Ethan watch as Laura Beth digs into a takeout container of lo mein. Time has passed. Conversations have been had. And Hope and Ethan are awaiting Laura Beth's response. But Laura Beth just eats. She's in control here. And she knows it.)

LAURA BETH. Good god. Thank you. This was the perfect choice. I needed this. MSG just hits different. Doesn't it? So fucking good. ... There any more egg rolls? Never mind, it's fine. ... Okay.

(Setting the container down, wiping her mouth with her sleeve. Hell, maybe a belch, here.)

Excuse me. So ... That's it?

HOPE. That's it. That's the deal.

LAURA BETH. Hell of a saleswoman.

HOPE. You know me.

LAURA BETH. Do I? Right, so to recap, if I may, my choices are... I cooperate with you against my will? Which nobody wants.

HOPE. No.

ETHAN. No.

LAURA BETH. I struggle and fail to escape, forcing you to kill me? Which, putting aside the fact that you don't want to, and the fact that I'm still not sure you even would, nobody wants. ... If I struggle and succeed in escaping?

HOPE. If you go to Harold, he will kill you. He wants you destroyed. He won't help you.

LAURA BETH. There are a lot of other places to go.

HOPE. He'll find you.

LAURA BETH. Will he?

ETHAN. Yes. He will.

LAURA BETH. Who the fuck is this guy? You two talk like he's the Moriarty to your Sherlock and Watson. Or would that be the other way around? Everyone's the protagonist of their own story, right?

HOPE. What matters is he will find you and kill you. Here, you're safe.

LAURA BETH. In a basement.

HOPE. You can have free reign of the house! At least with us you get to live.

LAURA BETH. For eight and a half months?

HOPE. The delivery won't kill you.

LAURA BETH. Just the part after it, right?

HOPE. ...

LAURA BETH. Let me ask you two a question. How do you think this is going to go? Put yourself in my shoes. You just found out everything you thought you knew is a lie. And your baby, upon birth, is gonna destroy mankind. Painfully. Wipe out the human race as we know it. Do you say "yes?" Yeah, sounds great!

HOPE. It's the right call.

LAURA BETH. Aha, no, I'm not convinced. Um--obviously, I don't want to die. But if I do, it's not like I'm gonna have any regrets. Didn't have time to make any. Much less realize them. But I bet the two of you have. So that's what I want to know. What happened to make you two so eager and excited to rush into your own deaths? And to want to drag literally everyone else in the world with you? That's what I'm still waiting for. Enlighten me.

HOPE. We told you.

LAURA BETH. Tell me again.

HOPE. ...

ETHAN. Humanity has run its course, Laura Beth.

LAURA BETH. ...

HOPE. He's right. We're killing the planet. We're killing each other. The world needs a clean slate. A fresh start. If we get a second chance, then it needs to be far away from the one we've botched now. We don't deserve this world anymore. This life. We're too cruel. And too deep.

LAURA BETH. That's a very high opinion of your fellow man.

HOPE. You've seen it.

LAURA BETH. Have I? Or is that just another thing you put up here? ... Maybe I should just kill you two because everybody else on the planet can't be fucking worse. ... I mean, you can't trust me. Not fully. Are you really gonna keep watch on me for the whole eight and a half yards? Sure you could lock me up again, but what if I stop eating? What happens? You gonna force feed me? Shovel lo mein down my throat? While I'm ripping out your hair? What if I bite your goddamn fingers off? What are you gonna do then? See, the right call--it's not mine to make. It's yours. I'm not the one who needs you in this transaction.

(Hope stands.)

Am I wrong?

HOPE. We will kill you. We don't want to. But if we have

to, we will.

LAURA BETH. *(nodding)* Mmm. Then do it.

(*Beat.*)

Do it.

(*Silence. Laura Beth leaps up and, with one hand, grabs Hope by the throat, choking her.*)

ETHAN. Woah!

LAURA BETH. *(seering into Hope)* If you are so unhappy and ugly inside that you want to die? I can grant you that now.

(*Ethan leaps up and tries to pull Laura Beth off. He can't. She is too strong. Her other arm keeps him at bay. She marvels at her own power.*)

Huh. You're both so weak.

(*Ethan bobs and weaves and manages to kiss Laura Beth on the mouth. This takes her back enough to release Hope, who falls to the ground, gasping for breath.*)

Hey, now. ... Well, I guess you did buy me dinner first.

ETHAN. Please stop.

(*Hope jumps up and punches Laura Beth. Laura Beth is moved, but unfazed. She punches Hope and Hope goes down. Beat. She kicks Hope while she's down.*)

Hey!

(*She kicks her again.*)

STOP!!

(*She kicks her again. Ethan grabs Laura Beth.*)

STOP IT!!

(*Again, Laura Beth is unfazed, but she allows Ethan's grab to pull her away. She turns to Ethan.*)

LAURA BETH. Kick her.

ETHAN. What?

LAURA BETH. Kick her. As hard as you can. In the face.

ETHAN. No.

LAURA BETH. If you really love me, you'll do it.

ETHAN. ...!

LAURA BETH. It's okay. Relax. It's okay, I'm just fucking with you.

(She sits back down and grabs the takeout container. She eats some more lo mein. Over the following, Hope struggles and slowly gets to her feet. Laura Beth speaks with mouthfuls of lo mein.)

That's the other thing, here, I still don't feel caught up on. What are--your feelings towards each other? Are you two married? Together?

ETHAN. Please don't.

LAURA BETH. Whatever the case, I can't imagine, Hope, it's easy for you knowing how good I've been fucking your man this whole time.

ETHAN. Laura Beth.

LAURA BETH. *(to Ethan)* Is it awkward for you? Probably not, right? More like every man's dream.

ETHAN. Stop. Talking.

(Beat.)

LAURA BETH. Okay. Touched a nerve. You got a look on your face, hubby.

(A dawning realization.)

Oh my god. You really love her. She couldn't do any of this without your help, could she? I hear the way she talks to you. Has the thought ever occurred, that maybe she's just using you?

ETHAN. Stop talking.

LAURA BETH. I bet she doesn't love you as much as you love her.

ETHAN. Stop.

LAURA BETH. Not as much as I did.

ETHAN. ...

LAURA BETH. I still could.

ETHAN. Please.

LAURA BETH. I'll love you. Kill her. Let's run away together. To the Adirondacks.

ETHAN. SHUT THE FUCK UP!

LAURA BETH. Let's see them for real.

(Hope, desperate, tunnel visioned, again tackles Laura Beth on her seat and attacks her ferociously, the unbridled rage in her soul making the purest physical appearance. To some degree, Laura Beth lets this happen. She's having the time of her life. Ethan tries to pull the two apart. The entire scene devolves into a violent scuffle. Eventually, Ethan manages to pull them apart. Infuriated by his interference, Hope punches Ethan, who goes down. Not out, but down. At the sight of this, Hope catches herself. She moves to check him.)

HOPE. Ethan?! Shit! Ethan?!

ETHAN. *(licking the wound)* I'm fine.

HOPE. Ethan? Are you--

ETHAN. Get off! I said I'm fine.

(He pushes her away and runs up the stairs, exiting.)

HOPE. Ethan! I'm sorry! Come back!

(But he's gone.)

LAURA BETH. *(laughing)* I'm right, aren't I? Oh my god.

(Hope sits, breathing hard.)

Shit, maybe he and I have more in common after all.
(Beat.)

HOPE. He's brilliant, you know. What he did with you? He explained to it me a thousand times, I barely understood a word.

LAURA BETH. He explained it to you? All I got was some humanoid bullshit.

(Hope laughs. Laura Beth does too. Silence.)

HOPE. What's it gonna take? For a yes?

LAURA BETH. Honestly? Probably nothing.

HOPE. You wanna see the mountains? For real? Grand Canyon. Niagara Falls? Anything. Name it. I'll take you wherever you want to go. Whatever you want to do. Swim in the ocean. Eat ice cream. Name it. What do you want?

LAURA BETH. Now that's the million-dollar question. Ain't it? What do I want? ... I kind of just want to get out of this fucking basement.

HOPE. Done. Where to?

LAURA BETH. Away from you, sweetie. You're the problem. It's not about anything you can do, it's you. I'm reasonably sure I hate you. I mean, who does the things you've done?

HOPE. I had to.

LAURA BETH. Don't say that.

HOPE. I had to. I didn't have a choice. I would have done this myself. Truly.

LAURA BETH. And yet, you didn't.

HOPE. Because I couldn't. I can't.

LAURA BETH. Why can't you?

HOPE. I can't, Laura Beth, I--I can't have children.

LAURA BETH. ...

HOPE. My tubes are tied. The way you can't fix.

LAURA BETH. ... Why the fuck would you do that?

HOPE. I didn't.

(Beat.)

Harold. Maybe you and I have more in common after all.

LAURA BETH. I'm sorry.

HOPE. I'm sorry, too. You didn't ask for this. Look, I should have told you from the beginning. I know that, now. I'm sorry. But the past is the past, I can't change it. I can only change right now. I'm not asking you to ignore what I've done. Only that you forgive me. What if we just--what if we just start over?

LAURA BETH. ... Okay. Sure. Hi, uh, my name, up until very recently used to be Laura Beth. What's yours?

HOPE. Hope.

LAURA BETH. Oh, that's a beautiful name. It's very nice to meet you, Hope. What is it that you do?

HOPE. I'm an editorial assistant.

LAURA BETH. Get the fuck out! I, too, until very recently was an editorial assistant. Small world.

HOPE. Small world.

LAURA BETH. Why an editorial assistant, anyway? I mean, why not just make me subservient from the beginning?

HOPE. *(That's an excellent question.)* Yeah. ... Because you deserve a choice. You deserve the choice.

LAURA BETH. But you weren't going to give it to me.

HOPE. No.

LAURA BETH. *(laughing)* ... You have no idea what the

fuck you're doing, do you?

HOPE. ...

LAURA BETH. ... I'll tell you what. You'll have my answer in eight and a half months.

(Laura Beth makes to leave.)

HOPE. Please.

LAURA BETH. I need to see the world for myself.

HOPE. Harold will find you. This is the only place we can protect you.

LAURA BETH. You already couldn't. You have to let me protect myself.

(Beat. Spotlights hit Laura Beth and Hope as the basement exits time. Laura Beth notices. Hope does not.)

Hmm.

(From somewhere nearby, perhaps even from her own clothes, Laura Beth pulls out Rodina's scarf and beret. She gives them to Hope.)

Here.

HOPE. What are these?

LAURA BETH. I don't need them anymore.

HOPE. ...

LAURA BETH. Don't beat yourself up. Okay? Children always do this to their parents.

(Beat. Then Hope bursts into teared laughter. Laura Beth offers a consoling hand. Then stands and ascends the stairs. But does stop halfway up.)

Last night. You asked me if I ever felt bad. ... I do.

(She exits.)

Hope is alone in her light, crying.

<u>SCENE EIGHT</u>

The ambience of an eager and attentive audience peppers itself in.

Snaps.

Hope notices the audience. She looks at the scarf and beret in her hands. Puts on the scarf. The beret. Her transformation is complete.

When ready, she begins.

RODINA (HOPE).
A painter told me once
"We create
To get closer to God
To help us bear the burden
Of our painful existence"

But do we?
Did he want a balm for his life?
Or just the attention?

I have lived in the dark
Where all our sins and orisons pour in and out of one another
Churning themselves into froth
A delectable milkshake that tastes so good but it's your least favorite flavor
A Root Beer float that's too sugary for your metabolism
A mug just straight up filled with semen and you're not someone into that sort of thing

IN THE SLUSH

You just want a cup of hot coffee with a flaky danish
Or a bottle of water with the perfect amount of
flouride
A lake and a sunrise
A good goddamn glass of red wine

That's all you want
Something that tastes better than semen
Or at least, something that you can see
Something easier to drown in

There is no "closer to God"
God's with us
Below
Trapped
Thrashing
Swallowing sea
Just trying to breathe
Breathe
Breathe
Breathe

Down here
We all meld together

Escape
Is only for the fortunate
The patient

(Rodina takes in a big gulp of air and holds her breath. Silence. A blacklight once again draws attention to the closed side room door, illuminating the same message. Or maybe it's been lit this whole time. Rodina turns and crosses to "THE CABINET" to exit.)

SULTRY ANNOUNCER (V.O.). Ladies and gentlemen.

(The door slams shut behind her, and she is gone, along with her light. "THE CABINET" burns alone, a light in the dark.)

Rodina Waits.

(Silence. "THE CABINET" light fades out. Darkness.)

<u>SCENE NINE</u>

Lights rise.

Some days later.

Perhaps some effort has been made to clean and straighten the basement, but it hasn't been that successful. Many papers and minutia still litter the room, as do new wine bottles and glasses.

No one is in the basement.

"THE CABINET" door is open.

No one is in the threshold.

After a moment, Hope enters from "THE CABINET," nursing a glass of wine. Maybe she's still wearing the scarf. She cleans and straightens, putting various papers back in boxes, emptying glasses or containers. She picks up one manuscript that makes her stop. It's the Becklesby Manuscript. She reads over it in silence, mulling it over.

The stairwell door opens, and Ethan's voice breaks her out of that world.

ETHAN (O.S.). Hope? You good?

HOPE. *(calling up)* Yeah! Come on down.

> *(She puts the manuscript wherever she deems it belongs as the voices of Ethan and Harold Becklesby are heard descending the stairs. Eventually, their bodies reveal themselves.)*

ETHAN (O.S.). You sure I can't offer you anything, Harold? Water? Tea?

HAROLD (O.S.). No. Thank you, Ethan. I'm fine.

ETHAN (O.S.). Suit yourself.

> *(As they reach the bottom, Hope and Harold lock eyes. Silence.)*

HAROLD. Hello, Hope.

HOPE. ... Dad. Sorry about the mess. Haven't really gotten a good chance to clean up yet.

HAROLD. That's quite all right.

HOPE. Sit. Please.

> *(They all sit.)*

You want a drink?

HAROLD. No. Thank you.

HOPE. I insist.

> *(She begins pouring two more glasses of wine.)*

HAROLD. Hope.

HOPE. No. We're drinking. I won't take no for an answer.

> *(She hands a glass to Ethan. He takes it. She hands a glass to Harold.)*

Here.

HAROLD. ...

> *(He takes the glass. Hope raises hers.)*

HOPE. A toast. To the end of yet another chapter. Prost.

> *(She finishes her glass. Ethan and Harold maybe drink. She tops herself off.)*

I have to hand it to you, Dad. Never in a million goddamn years did I see that coming. The balls on that move! It should not have worked.

HAROLD. I regret that I had to resort to such measures. But you left me with no alternative.

HOPE. I mean, Christ, you could have left us the fuck alone. We would have preferred that.

HAROLD. You know I couldn't.

HOPE. Yes. I know. I know very well that you couldn't. Did you actually want something or did you just come by to gloat?

HAROLD. Neither. I came to return the body.

HOPE. ...

HAROLD. I thought it the most respectable course of action. Given the circumstances. It is my understanding, given the marital status you gave her, you might wish to--

HOPE. Where is she?

HAROLD. The back of my van.

HOPE. You make it painful?

HAROLD. No more than I could avoid.

HOPE. ... Okay. Bye, then.

ETHAN. ...

HAROLD. I would inquire, if you are planning a service, I should like to attend.

HOPE. You won't be invited.

HAROLD. Very well.

HOPE. Get out.

HAROLD. Hope...

HOPE. What else is there to say?

HAROLD. Would you hear me?

HOPE. Hear you what? Say the same goddamn thing you say every time? No. I'm saving us the time. I'm tired. You're tired.

HAROLD. I am tired. I implore the both of you. You must reconsider your position in these matters. The Second Coming must never be brought unto us.

HOPE. There it is. Shocker. You want us to go back to

saving the world?

HAROLD. I would settle for no longer trying to destroy it.

HOPE. Yeah, well...1 ooks like we still have differing opinions on what that is, don't we?

HAROLD. It would seem. *(to Ethan)* Would you excuse us a moment, lad?

ETHAN. Um.

HOPE. It's okay. We won't be long.

ETHAN. Sure. I'll, uh, go get her. I guess.

(He stands and ascends the stairs, exiting.)

(Beat.)

HOPE. If you're just going to say the same thing, though--

HAROLD. Stop! Stop this, for the love of God.

HOPE. No.

HAROLD. Why?

HOPE. Because I don't want to.

HAROLD. You petulant fucking child. What did I do?

HOPE. What did you do?

HAROLD. ...

HOPE. Are you serious? What "DID YOU DO?!"

HAROLD. I did not mean that.

HOPE. YOU DID EVERYTHING TO ME! You woke me at the crack of dawn to read scriptures. You made me train in martial arts after school instead of making friends. You forbade me from talking to anybody other than you. You beat me if I questioned you. You drove mom away. You robbed me of--! ... You treated me like a thing instead of your daughter.

(Beat.)

HAROLD. I know I was not a good father. And for what it's

worth, I am truly sorry. I regret it. But being a proper parent is not the most important thing when the cosmic balance of the world is in jeopardy.

HOPE. ...!

HAROLD. I am sorry that my actions warped you in ways that I couldn't anticipate. But I did not intend nor ever imagine you would stray so far from everything I tried to teach you.

HOPE. Oh, well, thank god you're sorry! You feel bad? Is this the part where I cry and we hug?

HAROLD. Goddamn it, this is the part where you let down your wall for a minute! Listen to the words I am saying, don't just deflect them or shake them off. Forget the rest of the world, forget that boy you've suckered into this folly, forget your damn ego and talk with me, father to daughter. ... I can't stand seeing you like this, Hope. This person you've become. I can hardly recognize the child I once rocked to sleep in my arms. I see just a woman with so much anger and hate pouring out of her. Towards everything and everyone. And yes, I know I am to blame for most of it. Maybe all of it. It should be me that suffers for that. You don't want to help me anymore? You never want to see me again? Fine. But to insist on becoming the enemy we've fought against for so long? I can't believe... I won't believe that deep down this is something you really want.

HOPE. Hell. Maybe I don't. But you don't want it. That's enough.

HAROLD. ... I can't change what I've done to you, Hope. I can only ask that you forgive me for it.

(Beat. The irony, finally, truly, irrevocably hits her. Hope laughs. It is an exquisitely layered laugh, filled

with fatigue, sadness, bitterness, toxicity, inevitability, bewilderment, and other fancy words one might find in an unsolicited manuscript.)

What?

HOPE. Nothing.

HAROLD. Hope.

HOPE. It's nothing.

(Beat. And the one-two punch:)

My god, wait, you...I couldn't put my finger on it. I read that fucking manuscript front to back. Again and again. You went through all that trouble. Warned her about Ethan. What she was. The baby. But you never said a single word about me.

(She laughs. Then laughs some more.)

That's funny. That's really funny. ... I will never forgive you. Whatever it takes. I will see this child into this world. And you are going to watch it happen. You are going to watch me make it happen. You will be there. Helpless. And in your last moments, you will realize that despite everything, all that you've done wasn't enough. And that your pathetic, useless life saved no one. ... Get the fuck out of my house.

(Silence. Harold stands. He ascends the stairs and exits. Hope lets out the tension, fighting back tears (or maybe they're just flowing) and downing the rest of her glass. Maybe the bottle. Silence. The stairwell door opens and Ethan descends the stairs. Hope tries to compose herself a little.)

ETHAN. Hey. He's gone.

HOPE. Good.

ETHAN. You need anything?

HOPE. No. I'm good.

(Ethan crosses to console Hope. Hope grasps him and holds tight.)

HOPE. I'm so sorry I hit you.

ETHAN. It's okay. I get it.

HOPE. I do love you, I love you so--

ETHAN. Hey, I know. All right? I love you, too.

HOPE. Do you think I'm my father?

ETHAN. Do I what?

HOPE. Am I my father? Am I a bad person?

(Beat.)

ETHAN. No. Hope. No.

HOPE. ...

ETHAN. ... So what now?

(Beat.)

HOPE. I can certainly think of a lot of things not to do. You were right. We should have been upfront from the beginning. No lying. Allow her to make the choice. To choose to join us. We can build her again. The right way. Better. Maybe there's something from the old body we can salvage. You brought her in, right?

ETHAN. Hold up. Just calm down.

HOPE. What? Why? We gotta move quick. This is a lot.

ETHAN. Just... hang on.

HOPE. You're still with me on this, right? I can't do this alone. I can't do it without you.

ETHAN. I know.

HOPE. So...?

ETHAN. ... Yeah. Um, I'll bring her down. Will you go clear the table in the lab?

HOPE. Yeah.

(Hope is off towards the side room door. She keeps talking as she moves into the room and out of sight. Ethan just sort of stays where he is, his mind elsewhere.)

HOPE (O.S.). You know, I can't believe I'm actually about to say this, but maybe this whole thing was actually a blessing in disguise. I think we just learned a lot. Everybody gets knocked down a couple times on the way to greatness, right? I feel really good. I feel great, actually. I love you, baby.

(Ethan hasn't heard her, his mind elsewhere.)

Baby?

ETHAN. …

(Hope appears in the side room threshold.)

HOPE. Hey.

(Ethan looks at Hope, broken out of his world.)

I love you.

ETHAN. Oh. … I love you too.

(Hope smiles and disappears once more into the side room. Ethan stands in place for another moment. He ascends the stairs and exits. Left in the basement, stacks upon stacks of hopes and dreams.)

END OF PLAY. MERCI.

Acknowledgements

For a play spiraling around the task of poring through the infinite pile of stories and words in order that the worthiest be granted the opportunity to reach more people, the irony of this being my first published full-length is not lost on me. Rodina's grinning somewhere.

Writing is so often lonely work, filled with imposter syndrome and self-doubt, and those who connect with and uplift our stories mean everything. I owe a great deal of thanks and my deepest gratitude to Jonathan Cook and Ghost Light Publications for not only finding "Slush" amidst the…well, you know, but vibing with it enough to take it under their wing and champion it. I would like to also mention:

-The team at The Skeleton Rep(resents) and their Craft Development Process, especially the watchful eye and challenging dramaturgical care provided by Emily Claire Schmitt, who helped shape this play into the form it is.
-Max Moline, a freelance director, and continuous advocate for this piece, constantly spurring me forward.
-Taylor Barrett Gaines, for help with the French language sections and tolerating all my questions.
-My family, for always supporting my wildest dreams, and never insisting I get a "real" job.
-And to my partner, colleague, and incredible wife, Allisyn, whose love and support for this play arguably outweighs my own, thank you for extending those to me as a person. I love you. I am not building humanoids in a locked room in our basement. We cannot afford a basement.

Finally, I cannot conclude any thanks without raising a glass to Mary Shelley, for every storyteller crafting tales of created meeting creator owes her some allegiance and inspiration. Without her, this play (and countless other stories) would not exist. Hopefully she's grinning somewhere too.

NOTES
(Use this space to make notes for your production)

GATHER BY THE GHOST LIGHT

ORIGINAL STORIES FOR RADIO THEATER

GATHER BY THE GHOST LIGHT is a storytelling podcast in radio theater format. Think of the Ghost Light as your campfire. Gather around and listen to stories from a variety of genres. Playwright Jonathan Cook and Devon McSherry are the hosts of the series and most of the stories you hear were originally written as short stage plays and they now have been adapted to audio plays with professional voice actors and immersive sound effects. The audio plays produced on this podcast give these talented playwrights an even wider audience for their stories. We welcome you to join us in this journey as we extend the voices of emerging playwrights!

Available wherever you get your podcasts!

For more information, please visit:

www.gatherbytheghostlight.com

Gather by the Ghost Light annual anthologies of audio plays produced on the podcast are all available through Ghost Light Publications!

BOBBY IS DEAD
by Marty Matfess

(2M, 3W, Dark Comedy)

Chris has been madly in love with his best friend Annie for years, but she's only been interested in dating everyone else but him. After Annie's recent break up with her boyfriend Bobby, Chris feels this may finally be what he needs to find his way into her heart, but just like that ... she's already moved on to another guy she met at a coffee shop. Being the good friend that he is, Chris has agreed to hang out with the new guy's visiting sister while they go out on a date. Oh, and let's not forget about Bobby. Turns out he's not taking the break up too well and Chris is now caught between an aggressive ex-boyfriend while having to keep new guy's sister company. A play about love, lust, and getting shot in the head.

ALL BARK, NO BITE
by Kara Emily Krantz

(2M, 3W, Comedy)

Charlotte and Eugene live a quiet, no-nonsense lifestyle surrounded by sudoku and argyle. Robert and Bella are boisterous and messy and ridiculously in love. Then there's the neighbor, Suzanne, who basically doesn't know what's going on, but definitely has something to say about it. Sure, relationships can be exciting! They can also be confusing, unexpected, and expose us to profound emotional risk. However, relationships are almost always worth exploring, and if we're willing to be vulnerable, can fill up the empty or wounded spaces in our hearts. And if that doesn't work? Well, get a dog.

KINGDUMB

by Jonathan Cook

(10M, 6W, Comedy)

There's a new King in the land that has initiated a mysterious new tax on the citizens. Outraged, the region's finest Clock fixer, aka "Time Repair Specialist", recruits some of the most unlikely rebels to help him develop a plan to overthrow the King. Their plotting takes them on a comedic journey through perilous mountain tops all the way to the palace itself where they confront this vile King face to face. Kingdumb is a medieval fantasy comedy full of absurdist humor and illogical behavior.

THE ROCK AND THE HARD PLACE

by Emily McClain

(4M, 3W, Modern Tragedy)

Alan Tully was convicted of the murder of Janice Beck in 1996 and has been on death row for 23 years, during which time he has maintained his innocence. His daughter Elsie receives a letter from the man who claims to have committed the crime and she attempts to use the information to exonerate her father. The insurmountable challenges of exonerating a wrongly convicted person drive her to the desperate position of threatening a man she believes could help free her father, with disastrous results.

www.ingramcontent.com/pod-product-compliance
Lightning Source LLC
Chambersburg PA
CBHW070344010826
48976CB00019B/2610